HOW DO
BEARS SLEEP?

HOW DO
BEARS SLEEP?

written and illustrated by E. J. Bird

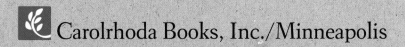
Carolrhoda Books, Inc./Minneapolis

This book is available in two editions:
Library binding by Carolrhoda Books, Inc.,
 a division of Lerner Publishing Group
Soft cover by First Avenue Editions,
 an imprint of Lerner Publishing Group
241 First Avenue North
Minneapolis, MN 55401 U.S.A.

Website address: www.lernerbooks.com

Library of Congress Cataloging-in-Publication Data

Bird, E. J.
  How do bears sleep?/written and illustrated by E. J. Bird
    p.   cm.
  Summary: Describes, in verse, what goes on in the bear's den during winter hibernation.
    ISBN 0–87614–384–2 (lib. bdg.)
    ISBN 0–87614–522–5 (pbk.)
    1. Bears—Hibernation—Juvenile literature. [1. Bears—Hibernation.] I. Title.
  QL737.C27B47 1990
  599.74'44604543—dc20   89–32370

Manufactured in the United States of America
8 9 10 11 12 13 – JR – 05 04 03 02 01 00

*For all children who are lucky enough
to have grandmothers like Nan,
my sweet wife and very special friend*

Author's Note

All living things have little clocklike gadgets buried somewhere inside telling them how fast to grow, when to get old, when to get hungry or sleepy—things like that.

Some animals, like squirrels and groundhogs and frogs and bears, have clocks that tell them it's high time they go to sleep all winter. That's right—ALL WINTER! And they find themselves someplace out of the weather, like a cave, and they really do go to sleep—that's called hibernating. And all the fat that they've stored up keeps them alive while they sleep.

There are lots of people who have uncovered nests of squirrels or dug frogs out of the mud in the wintertime, but not many go snooping around where the bears are sleeping.

I've often wondered what goes on in that cave with the bears—haven't you?

The north wind is stirring
And dry leaves are shifting,
Soon you'll see snow
A-blowing and drifting.

This is the time
When winter comes creeping,

And this is the time
When a bear thinks of sleeping.

Needing a cave,
He'll search high and low
Till finally he finds one
To keep out the snow.

Now I've asked all my friends
But nobody knows
Just how a bear sleeps
When the winter wind blows.

Does he make up a bed
Of dry leaves and stones,
Or lie on the ground
Just resting his bones?

Does he sleep on his belly
Or flat on his back?
With his mouth opened wide
Or just opened a crack?

Does he twist? Does he turn?
Does he snarl and get grumpy?
Does he tear up his bed
When it starts feeling lumpy?

Does he lie very still,
Without any twitching,
Or lift up a paw
To scratch where it's itching?

Is part of his time
Spent arranging the boulders
To keep the sharp edges
From scuffing his shoulders?

Does he stare, eyes wide open,
Without ever blinking,
Or shut his eyes tight
To help while he's thinking?

Does he squint in the dark,
Lying still in his bed?
Does he rub his brown eyes
Till his brown eyes are red?

Does he curl in a ball?
Does he whimper or snore?
Does he have scary dreams
And wake up with a roar?

Or maybe he dreams
Of grubs under logs
Or cool summer evenings
And the croaking of frogs.

Maybe it's strawberries,
All squashy and dripping,
With juices so runny
They're just made for sipping.

Or high mountain meadows
With a clean south wind blowing,
The clouds white like lace
And wildflowers growing.

Or a soft summer night,
Crickets sawing a tune,
And a whisper of wind
And a slice of a moon.

Does he dream of sweet cherries
And old honey trees?
Combs dripping with honey
And no honeybees?

Now here are some problems—
It doesn't seem right—
How does he sleep
When it's not even night?

How can he miss Christmas
Or New Year's horns blaring?
How can he lie there
Without even caring?

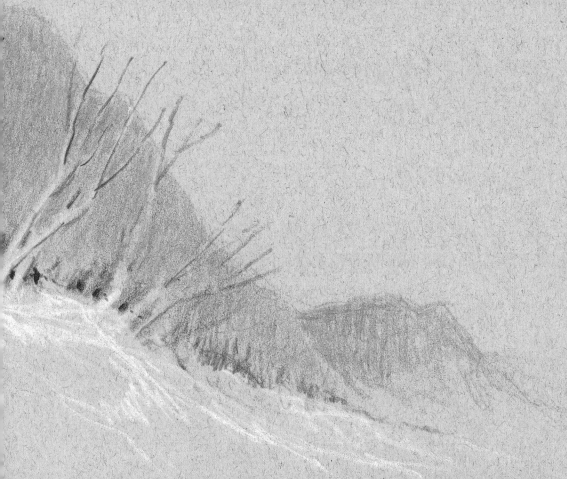

How can he sleep
Through a wild, howling blizzard
Or a cold, driving wind
That freezes his gizzard?

A bleary-eyed bear
All droopy and dozy
In his snow-drifted cave,
Can his fur keep him cozy?

Try to imagine
Or even to think—
From November to April
Without even a drink!

If I live to be ninety
I'm sure I won't know
How a bear sleeps
Through the cold winter snow.

'Cause I'm sure it would be
A horrendous mistake
To go poking around
And find him AWAKE!

ABOUT THE AUTHOR
AND ILLUSTRATOR

E. J. Bird was born on a rocky one-man farm in the foothills of Utah. As a small boy, he always had plenty of animals to play with. He had pet colts, calves, dogs, and roosters. He once had a magpie that could talk and a black lamb that would pull him around in a little wooden cart. As he grew older, he began to draw the creatures around him, and he learned how to tell when they looked right or wrong on the canvas. Mr. Bird has worked as a ranch hand and as a professional artist, and he still loves to watch animals—especially bears. He is the author and illustrator of the Carolrhoda titles TEN TALL TALES and CHUCK WAGON STEW.